By Isabel Gaines
Illustrated by Studio Orlando

First published by Parragon in 2012
Parragon
Queen Street House
4 Queen Street
Bath BA1 1HE, UK
www.parragon.com

ISBN 978-1-4454-4750-6

Printed in China

Disney Winnie the Pooh

Easter Egg Hunt

little story for little learners

Bath • New York • Singapore • Hong Kong • Cologne • Delhi
Melbourne • Amsterdam • Johannesburg • Auckland • Shenzhen

"Happy Easter!"
Winnie the Pooh
called to his friends.

It was time for
the Easter egg hunt.

Rabbit said,

"Whoever finds the

most eggs wins.

Get ready,

get set...go!"

Pooh, Piglet,
Roo, Eeyore
and Kanga walked
into the woods.

Pooh found a yellow egg
under some daffodils.
He put the egg
in his basket.

But Pooh did not know
his basket had a hole.
The egg fell out
onto the grass.

Piglet found
Pooh's yellow egg.
"Lucky me!" he said.

Then Pooh found
a purple egg
behind a rock.
That egg slipped out, too!

Roo found Pooh's egg.
"Oh, goody!" he cried.
"Purple is my
favourite colour!"

Pooh found a green
egg and put it in his
basket. But he did not
see it fall out.

Tigger found
Pooh's green egg.
"I am on my way
to winning!" he said.

Pooh found a red egg.
It fell through the
hole, too.

Eeyore found
Pooh's red egg.
"Oh, my," he said.
"I found one."

On the side of a hill,
Pooh found a blue egg.
"How pretty!" he said.

Kanga found
Pooh's blue egg
next to a log.

"Time is up!"

Rabbit shouted.

Everyone ran over

to see who had won.

Pooh looked inside
his empty basket.
"My eggs seem to be
hiding again," he said.

Piglet looked at the basket.
He poked his hand
through the hole.
'I think I know why,"
said Piglet.

"You can have my
yellow egg," said Piglet.
"It was probably your eg
before it was mine."

"Thank you, Piglet,"
said Pooh.
"And you can have my
purple egg," said Roo.

"Here, Buddy Bear,"
said Tigger.
"Tiggers like to win fa
and square."

Eeyore gave Pooh
his red egg.
"It was too good to be
true," said Eeyore.
Kanga said,
"Take mine, Pooh!"

Rabbit counted the eggs.

"Pooh is the winner!"

he cried.

"You win an Easter feast

The feast was great fun.
Everyone ate Easter eggs!
But Pooh liked
the honey best!